SLAP-SHOT
SLUMP

BY JAKE MADDOX

text by
Brandon Terrell

STONE ARCH BOOKS
a capstone imprint

Jake Maddox JV books are published by Stone Arch Books
A Capstone Imprint
1710 Roe Crest Drive
North Mankato, Minnesota 56003
www.capstonepub.com

Library of Congress Cataloging-in-Publication Data

Maddox, Jake, author.
  Slap-shot slump / by Jake Maddox ; text by Brandon Terrell.
    pages cm. -- (Jake Maddox JV)
  Summary: At his old school fourteen-year-old Simon Wahlberg was the best player on
his hockey team, but when he tries out for the Edgewater High School's varsity team he
discovers that the competition is pretty fierce — and not just on the ice.
  ISBN 978-1-4342-9635-1 (library binding) -- ISBN 978-1-4342-9667-2 (pbk.) -- ISBN 978-1-4965-
0176-9 (ebook PDF)
1. Hockey stories. 2. Competition (Psychology)--Juvenile fiction. 3. Self-confidence--
Juvenile fiction. 4. High schools--Minnesota--Juvenile fiction. 5. Friendship--Juvenile
fiction. [1. Hockey--Fiction. 2. Competition (Psychology)--Fiction. 3. Self-confidence--Fiction.
4. High schools--Fiction. 5. Schools--Fiction. 6. Friendship--Fiction. 7. Minnesota--Fiction.] I.
Terrell, Brandon, 1978- author. II. Title.

 PZ7.M25643Slp 2015
 813.6--dc23

                          2014022991

This book has been officially leveled by using the F&P Text Level Gradient™
Leveling System.

Art Director: Heather Kindseth
Designer: Veronica Scott
Production Specialist: Jennifer Walker

Photo Credits:
Shutterstock: mariakraynova, chapter openings, photographer2222, cover, Pressmaster, back
cover
Design Elements: Shutterstock

Printed in China by Nordica.
0914/CA21401508
092014   008470NORDS15

TABLE OF CONTENTS

CHAPTER 1

TRYOUTS

"Here goes nothing," fourteen-year-old Simon Wahlberg said under his breath. He stood outside the hockey arena, his huge equipment bag slung over his shoulder, staring up at a sign over the door. It read: EDGEWATER ICE ARENA. HOME OF THE BLIZZARDS!

Simon's dad stepped up beside him and clapped him on the shoulder with one massive hand. "You'll do great, kiddo," he said.

Simon wished he shared his father's confidence. Today was tryout day for Edgewater

High School's varsity hockey team. Simon and his parents had just moved to Edgewater from a small town in southern Minnesota so that Simon could have the best possible hockey training. Edgewater was known for its championship hockey team. They were considered the best in the state, and making the team was extremely difficult.

Together, Simon and his dad entered the ice arena. A blast of cool air hit them as they walked through the door.

The arena was already buzzing with kids. On the ice, a number of players — some wearing Blizzards' jerseys, others in white practice jerseys with numbers pinned to them — skated in circles or lazily hit pucks to one another.

"There's Coach Burke," Simon's dad said. He pointed to a man standing near the scorekeeper's bench studying a clipboard. The coach looked to be in his late twenties and had close-cropped black hair.

At the far end of the arena was a door that led to the boys' locker room. As Simon and his dad approached, the door banged open and three kids exited. They towered over Simon. The one in the lead, a boy with a square jaw and a crooked nose, sneered at Simon as he passed. The back of his jersey read BUCKLEY, and there was a large *C* on one sleeve.

He must be the team captain, Simon thought. He watched as the three boys stepped onto the ice and skated away.

"This is it," Simon's dad said. "Good luck, bud."

"Thanks, Dad," Simon said, pushing his way into the locker room to get ready.

The locker room smelled like sour sweat, but Simon was used to it. Every locker room he'd ever been in had had that same scent. He found an open spot on a wooden bench, changed into his pads, taped up his stick, laced his skates tight, and let out a deep, nervous breath.

"You got this, Simon," he whispered to himself before heading out to the rink.

Usually when his skates hit the ice, Simon's nerves went away. But not today. As he pushed off toward the center red line, where Coach Burke was gathering the players, Simon noticed that he was the smallest kid on the ice by far.

It makes sense, Simon thought. *I'm a freshman after all, and most of these guys are probably at least sophomores.*

Once most of the group had gathered, Coach Burke called out, "Let's do a few minutes of skating to warm up!"

Simon began skating around the rink, and eventually it put him a little at ease. Skating was his strongest skill.

After about five minutes, Coach stopped the warm-up and split the players up into groups of twelve. "We're going to do some sprints now — get those legs moving," Coach Burke said.

When it was Simon's turn, his group started on the red line at the end of the rink — the goal line. Simon bent his knees in the ready position. Coach Burke blew the whistle, and the group pushed off toward the opposite goal line. Simon dug his blades into the ice and took off like a shot. His strides were quick and easy, and he was the first in his group to reach the goal line.

After a few rounds of sprints, Coach gathered the group up again. "Now we'll do some agility work. See how quickly you can change direction, stop, get going again," he explained. "I want you to skate around until you hear my whistle, then stop. When you hear a second whistle, you'll change directions."

Coach Burke also had each player showcase his cornering and crossovers. Cornering was difficult, but Simon had been practicing it for years. In order to turn sharply, you had to lean your body weight to one side. To pick up speed while doing this, you had to place one skate in front of the other, or "crossover," while leaning from one side to the other.

Coach tested these skills by having the players skate around one of the goals, and then maneuver through a series of orange cones. Simon made it look effortless. As he passed Coach Burke, he heard the man say, "Nicely done."

When they'd finished their skating drills, Coach Burke split the players up into groups of three. Simon found himself in the same group as the team captain and another player with long, shaggy hair.

"Hey, I'm Simon," he said, introducing himself.

"What's up? I'm Kent," the shaggy-haired boy said.

"Grant," the captain added, not bothering to say hello. "Let's try not to mess this up, okay?"

Before Simon could figure out if Grant was being serious, their trio was up. They took their turn skating the length of the rink, passing the puck between them, and displaying their stickhandling abilities.

Simon could barely keep up with his two partners. When he had an opportunity to shoot into the open net, Simon launched a wrist shot that clanged off the goal post and skittered away across the ice.

Grant snickered unkindly as he skated past Simon. "Nice shot," he said.

He's definitely not joking, Simon thought.

By the time Coach Burke released everyone, Simon was exhausted and frustrated. He pulled his helmet off and wiped the sweat from his forehead with one glove.

At my old school, it was clear I was the best player on the team, Simon thought as he skated off the ice. *But in Edgewater? I'm just a small fish in a big, frozen pond.*

CHAPTER 2

ON THE ROSTER

It had been two Saturdays since Simon's hockey tryout and a whole month since his family had moved to their new home in Edgewater, but Simon's room was still cluttered with cardboard boxes. *I guess it's about time I unpack,* Simon thought as he sat up in bed that morning, yawning and stretching his arms and legs.

The only things he'd bothered to unpack so far were his hockey trophies, which took up three shelves on his giant bookcase, and a few posters of hockey legends like Bobby Orr and Gordie Howe.

Simon slowly got out of bed and walked across his room to a stack of cardboard boxes. Opening up the box at the top of the pile, Simon found his favorite poster — a framed image of a hockey puck with the numbers 24/7/365 printed on the puck in white ink.

This will be perfect right above my bed, Simon thought as he held the frame in front of him, admiring it.

Hockey was Simon's life.

Ever since he'd strapped on his first pair of skates at the age of five, Simon had been in love with the sport. He loved the feeling of his blades on the ice, how it felt like he was gliding through the air. He loved the feeling he got when he slipped the hockey puck past a goalie and into the net.

From an early age, it was clear that Simon had a natural talent for hockey. At his old school, he'd been the team's starting center and captain. He had skated circles around his competition.

Simon's parents had decided that if he wanted to succeed at a more challenging level, they needed to move somewhere that had an elite hockey program. Edgewater was the clear choice.

And so here he was, in a new school, a new town, and a new bedroom, uncertain about whether or not he'd made the team.

School had started last week. Simon had hated the first day. He'd been the center of attention in each class — clearly one of the only ninth-grade students who hadn't attended Edgewater Middle School. In every class, Simon had been asked to stand and say his name and something about himself while the whole class stared at him. For the most part, he'd just said, "I love hockey," or, "I met Wayne Gretzky once."

He had made a friend — a guy named Mike Starkey who sat next to Simon in science class. Mike lived pretty close to Simon, but they hadn't met up to hang out after school yet.

Simon had seen Coach Burke around school a few times, mostly in the cafeteria and gymnasium. Each time Simon had seen the coach, he'd wanted to run over and ask if he'd made the team.

I wonder how much longer I'll have to wait to find out, he thought as he searched the box for a hockey puck Wayne Gretzky had signed for him when Simon had met him a few years back.

"Hey, Simon," his dad said, appearing in the doorway of his bedroom and interrupting his thoughts. A pair of Rollerblades dangled from one hand. "Want to go around the block with me and get some fresh air?"

"Absolutely," Simon said. *Sitting around waiting for the phone to ring is worse than watching paint dry,* he thought. *This will be a good distraction.*

"Great! I'll meet you outside," Dad said.

Simon put on some jeans and joined his dad on the front steps. After strapping on a pair of

Rollerblades and a helmet, he and his dad skated down the sloping driveway and out onto the street.

"See if you can catch up!" Dad shouted, laughing. He skated down the street, carving back and forth with ease. Simon took off after him.

Simon's dad had played hockey when he was younger, and he'd always been encouraging of Simon's decision to play the sport.

Heck, he and Mom even switched jobs and moved to a new house and town all because they want me to succeed at hockey, Simon thought. It was a sacrifice he did not take for granted.

Simon and his dad skated along smoothly paved roads. Their neighborhood was still being developed, and they passed several new constructions.

A few blocks from their house was a large park. On one side, near a pair of fenced-in tennis courts, the city had built a small wooden ice rink. It was still too early in the fall for the rink to be filled with ice. During the winter, though, it would probably be packed with kids.

I can't wait until I can do this on the ice there, Simon thought as he whipped around and glided backward beside his dad. He'd practiced for a long time in order to master this tough skill — and earned a lot of bruises and scrapes along the way.

"Remember," Dad said, "balance is key. It's the most important part of hockey." He increased his speed and wove around Simon, trying to break his concentration. Simon wasn't having it. He handled the added pressure with ease.

They skated a couple of laps around the new neighborhood, and for the time being, Simon forgot all about the hockey tryouts. That is, until they skated up their driveway and saw Simon's mom standing on the steps, the phone in her hand.

Mom waved excitedly for Simon, then spoke into the phone. "You know what, Coach Burke? He just got home."

Simon raced up the driveway, skidding to a stop next to his mom. He took the phone from her.

"Hello?" Simon said breathlessly. His heart thumped so loudly in his chest, he was afraid the coach might hear it over the phone.

"Simon!" Coach Burke sounded pleased to hear his voice. "I've got some good news for you. We'd officially like to have you on the team. What do you think?"

"Um, yeah," Simon croaked, hardly able to believe it. "I'd love that."

"Perfect!" the coach replied. "First practice is Monday morning. Five thirty a.m. Got it?"

"Got it," Simon said. "Thanks, Coach."

"Welcome to the Blizzards, Simon," Coach Burke said.

Simon hung up the phone, then pumped his fist in the air.

"That's our all-star!" Dad said, wrapping Simon's mom in a giant bear hug.

CHAPTER 3

THE FIRST PRACTICE

"Man, it's early," Simon said on Monday morning as he wiped the sleep from his eyes and hopped out of Dad's car. It was still dark outside, and Simon was chilled by the brisk fall air.

"Have a great practice," Dad said as Simon lugged his equipment bag out of the backseat.

"Thanks," Simon said. He hefted the bag over one shoulder and walked through the same doors he'd first entered two weeks ago.

Simon was so excited for the first hockey practice, he had barely slept a wink the night before. That's why he was dragging his feet now. Thankfully, he'd stashed a protein bar in his bag. *That should give me some energy,* he thought.

In the locker room, a couple of his new teammates were also suiting up. As Simon sat down and started to put his shoulder pads on, a tall, rail-thin boy came over. "Hey! Who's the new kid?" he asked.

"Um, Simon Wahlberg," Simon introduced himself.

"Nice to meet you, Simon," the boy said. He offered a hand, and Simon shook it. "Blake Vaughn, left wing." He pointed to a kid seated nearby on a bench. "And that's Quentin Jasper. Right wing."

Quentin was stocky and had a shock of unruly brown hair that made it look like he'd just gotten out of bed. Since it wasn't even six in the morning yet, he probably just had. He looked up from lacing his skates. "'Sup," he said.

"He's much friendlier after he's been on the ice," Blake whispered. Then he added, "Don't be too intimidated by these goofs. We don't bite." He thought for a second. "Well, maybe Grant does. No promises there."

Simon smiled. "I'll keep that in mind," he said.

"Well, see you on the ice, Simon," Blake said as he rapped his knuckles on Simon's shoulder pads. Quentin joined him, and the two headed toward the locker room exit.

Simon hurried to put on his skates. He grabbed his hockey stick — the old wooden one he'd used for years — and made his way to the rink.

There were a total of twenty-three players on the team, and Simon was the only ninth grader. Many of the guys on the team had new gear: shiny skates and lightweight, carbon-fiber sticks.

Everyone on the team looked like they'd been playing together since they were kids. The way they skated together was easy and effortless.

Simon suddenly felt like a monkey wrench messing up a team of well-oiled gears.

Simon started skating around the rink to warm up. Some of the other guys did the same. Coach Burke stood at center ice. Next to him stood a short man in a blue jacket with the name "Martin" stitched on the sleeve. A cardboard box sat beside them on the ice.

Coach Burke blew his whistle. "Bring it in, Blizzards!" His voice echoed off the empty arena's walls. The team skated to center ice and huddled together. Simon got stuck in the back of the pack and had a hard time seeing past the shoulders in front of him. "Coach Martin here has your jerseys."

"Grant Buckley!" Coach Martin yelled in a nasally voice. The huge captain with the crooked nose reached out and caught his jersey.

One by one, the jerseys were handed out. When Simon's name was called, he raised his hand. "Back here!" he called.

Simon tried to press his way between the two kids in front of him, but they barely budged. Somehow he managed to catch the jersey Coach Martin threw his way. It was blue with yellow stripes. On the back was his number — 11.

Simon slid the jersey on. He was finally starting to feel like part of the team.

Coach Burke broke the team up into four lines. Each line consisted of a center, two wings, and two defensemen. Simon was disappointed when he was placed on the fourth line. While the first and second lines were made up of the team's best scorers, the fourth line was considered the "energy line." They basically gave the other players time to rest. And while the fourth-line players were excellent skaters, they received the least amount of game time and scored the fewest goals.

Well, Simon thought, *what did I expect? I'm the youngest guy here and probably the only one who's never played with any of these other guys.*

Coach Martin placed a row of orange cones on the ice, and they started with stickhandling and puck-control drills. Each player wove between the cones, dribbling a puck with his stick and alternating between using his forehand and backhand. At the end of the cones was the goal protected by the team's starting goalie, Nate Singh.

Simon watched as Grant wove through the cones and hit a perfect slap shot. The puck sizzled past Nate's leg and into the net.

"Nice shot, Captain!" a voice called out.

The rest of the first line, including the two defensemen, Howie and Tim, took turns next. Each of them made the drill look like a piece of cake.

When it was Simon's turn, he dribbled the puck with his blade and hit the cones fast, weaving between them. His nerves made the stick shake in his hands, though, and on the second pass with his backhand, the puck skittered away from him.

Simon tried to recover, but he hit a cone with his front skate and fell hard to the ice.

"That's all right, Simon," Coach Burke barked. "Get up, keep at it."

Simon raised himself up. He could hear someone snickering and looked up to see Grant covering his mouth as he laughed. Simon grabbed his stick off the ice and brought the puck back to the course.

As he continued though, Simon was more timid. He moved slowly, afraid he was going to crash again. When he reached the end, his weak wrist shot was easily gobbled up by Nate's giant goalie mitt.

Simon was humiliated. He wanted to impress the team, not embarrass himself in front of them.

I know I can do better, Simon thought. *I need to step up my game. If I'm going to play for the Blizzards, I'll have to work harder than I ever have before.*

CHAPTER 4

TEAMING UP

"All right, everybody. Let's split into teams of three to begin our group projects," Simon's science teacher, Ms. Mayhew, said the following Wednesday. She studied her students sternly. According to his new friend Mike, no one could remember the last time she actually smiled in class. She was even more intimidating than Coach Burke.

Simon was exhausted after his first few practices with the Blizzards. But hearing the phrase "group project" made him perk up. He began to scan the classroom. A lot of kids had already teamed up with their friends. They started pulling their desks together right away, metal legs scraping loudly against the floor.

Simon turned and made eye contact with Mike across the room. His friend waved him over. Simon found a blue plastic chair, set it beside Mike's desk, and plopped down in it.

A girl with thick black glasses and dark hair walked over to them, and Simon tried to remember her name. *Is it Maya? Mariah?* He'd spent every waking second thinking about hockey lately and hadn't been paying much attention to the rest of the students in his classes.

"Mind if I join your team, Mike?" the dark-haired girl asked.

"Of course, Kaya," Mike said.

Kaya, Simon thought. *That's it.*

Kaya turned an open desk to face Mike and Simon and sat down.

Simon smiled at her. "Hi, I'm Simon," he introduced himself.

She smiled back. "Kaya."

"Okay, listen up, everyone," Ms. Mayhew said. "I'll be going around the room and assigning topics. Your team must then discuss the topic outside of class, come up with an investigation to complete, create a hypothesis, and write a report based on what you find."

"We should totally meet up tonight to go over our ideas for the assignment," Mike said as Ms. Mayhew began walking around the room. He was oddly excited about homework.

Kaya shrugged. "The public library is open until nine," she suggested.

"Wanna meet up after dinner?" Mike asked.

Simon had to think about it for a second. His hockey schedule was very demanding. Unlike some of the other teams, which had to share the ice with other winter sport activities, Edgewater's varsity hockey team had its own facility. They practiced as much as they could.

"I have practice until six or so," Simon said. "But I could come to the library after I'm done."

"Great!" Mike said enthusiastically.

Ms. Mayhew finally stopped at Simon's group. "Your topic will be . . ." Ms. Mayhew checked her notes. "The relationship between force and mass."

"Thank you, Ms. Mayhew," Mike said, scribbling the topic into his spiral notebook.

"So . . . library tonight, then?" Kaya asked. "Should we meet at seven?"

"I'll be there," Mike said.

"Simon?" Kaya asked.

Simon nodded. "Absolutely," he said. "Seven o'clock. I'll be there."

* * *

That afternoon's practice was tough. Coach Burke ran the team through a number of passing and zone drills. Simon had been working extra hard to make sure the coaches saw his progress. Even so, he was still on the fourth line.

By the time they were released, Simon was a sore, aching mess. Every muscle in his body burned. He took longer than usual to change out of his pads, and it was nearly seven o'clock when he shoved the last of his gear into his equipment bag. That gave him very little time to walk the half-mile to the public library and stop to get something to eat on the way there.

Simon was just about out the door when Blake stopped him. "Hey, man," he said. "Where are you dashing off to? Hot date tonight?"

"Oh," Simon said. "Just . . . I have a thing."

"A thing?" Blake repeated. "That's nice and specific."

Simon chuckled.

"Bummer," Blake continued. "Some of the guys are coming over to my house. We're gonna play some Xbox, maybe order some pizza."

Simon almost groaned. This was the first time any of the other players had invited him to hang out. He hated to pass up the opportunity. *Who knows if they'll invite me again if I don't go?* he thought. *Plus, our first game's coming up next week, and I want to feel as much a part of the team as I can.*

"Quentin, Howie, and Nate are coming," Blake continued. "Grant was going to come, but he's got to get to his job working as an angry statue in a water fountain." Blake scowled in a perfect imitation of Grant.

Simon weighed his options. He hated to cancel on his first group meeting for the science project. But on the other hand, he knew they had plenty of time to finish their assignment. *It's not a huge deal if I skip this one meeting,* he told himself.

"You know," Simon said, "my thing's not that important. I mean, not as important as pepperoni and a little Xbox."

Blake smiled. "Cool, man. Let me get my gear. You can hitch a ride with me."

As he waited for Blake outside the locker room, Simon pulled out his phone typed up a quick text to Mike. *Something came up,* he wrote. *Can't make it 2 library. Sorry.*

* * *

While Simon was playing video games and eating pizza with his hockey teammates that night, he got a text back from Mike.

Be at the library Saturday at 9:00 a.m., he wrote. *We have a lot of work to do.*

Simon felt bad for bailing on his group project but glad he was able to hang with his teammates.

If I hadn't hung out with them tonight, they probably wouldn't have invited me again, he thought. *Besides, what's Mike so worried about? The project's not even due till Monday.*

With that, Simon sat back, grabbed another slice of pizza, and waited his turn to play Xbox.

CHAPTER 5

FACE-OFF

It had been a tiring week, so Saturday morning, Simon slept in. Practice was late that afternoon so he had plenty of time to lounge . . . or at least he thought he did.

Around noon, Simon finally sat up in bed and checked his phone. *Five missed calls? That's strange,* he thought, staring at the screen. *And they're all from Mike?*

Suddenly Simon started to panic. *Oh, no,* he realized. *Today's Saturday. I was supposed to meet Mike and Kaya at the library at nine to work on the report. I'm the worst! How could I have forgotten?*

Simon jumped out of bed and threw on his clothes as fast as he could. He ran to the kitchen, grabbed a granola bar, and bolted around the corner to the front hallway, nearly running smack into his mom.

"Whoa! What are you — " she began to ask.

"Can't talk, Mom!" Simon shouted. "I gotta meet my science group at the library!" He sprinted to the door, ran out to the garage, and hopped on his bike. Simon pedaled fast in the direction of the library, which was about a mile down the road.

But when Simon arrived ten minutes later, he couldn't find his friends anywhere. He searched the first floor, then the second.

They're already gone, Simon thought, his heart sinking.

Just then, Simon felt his phone buzz in his coat pocket. A text from Mike.

Kaya and I worked hard on our parts this morning, Mike wrote. *Make sure you get yours done by Monday.*

Simon felt horrible. But hockey practice would be starting in about an hour, so he headed back home to get ready.

* * *

The first hockey game of the season was at home that Tuesday. There was an extra buzz to the locker room beforehand. Loud heavy metal music blasted throughout the space. Quentin, normally a quiet guy, sang along loudly, banging his fists against the metal lockers to the beat, pumping himself up.

Simon wrapped a line of tape around the grip of his hockey stick, bobbing his head to the beat of the music. His stomach was twisted in knots, and he felt like he might throw up.

Keep calm. It's only a game, he thought, trying to settle his nerves.

It wasn't working.

"Listen up, everyone!" Coach Burke shouted over the music. One of the guys muted the sound, and the locker room suddenly became quiet.

"Wear those jerseys with pride today, boys," Coach continued. "Give it everything you've got, and this game is ours. Now . . . are you ready to play?"

They all responded with a booming, "Yes, sir!"

"Then let's go win us a hockey game!" Coach Burke shouted.

The boys hooted and hollered, and Simon joined in, feeling a wave of team spirit wash over him. They burst from the locker room and into an arena filled with cheering fans.

Simon was amazed at how many people, most dressed in Blizzards' blue and yellow, were in the stands. Simon spotted his parents sitting beside the school pep band. His mom waved frantically when he saw her.

The announcer ran through both teams' rosters. First, he introduced the players on the opposing team, the Granville Vultures. Then he ran down the Blizzards' lineup.

When the announcer called out Simon's name, he skated to center ice, hand raised to the cheering crowd. It was a rush like nothing he'd ever experienced.

The first line — Grant at center, Blake at left wing, Quentin at right, and Tim and Howie playing defense — stayed out on the ice while the rest of the team skated to the bench.

Grant looked intimidating as he stood hunched over in the face-off circle at center ice. He chewed on his plastic mouth guard and stared down the Vultures' center who stood across from him.

"Let's go, Blizzards!" Simon shouted from the bench.

Grant won the face-off. He slapped the puck to Blake, who handled it perfectly. A Vultures' defender raced up and jabbed at the puck, but Blake passed it across the ice to Quentin before the defender got to it. Quentin curled around the back of the goal and flicked the puck out to Grant.

Grant wound up, his stick unleashing a loud crack throughout the arena as it struck the puck. The puck rocketed forward. The goalie barely got his glove up in time to pluck the shot out of the air before it passed into the net.

Simon was in awe watching his teammates. *Sure, they were impressive at practice,* he thought, *but now they're kicking it up a notch.*

Later in the first period, after Howie intercepted a pass and cleared it into the neutral zone, Grant and Blake surged toward the goal. They passed the puck back and forth until Grant came to a sudden stop and launched the puck into the upper corner of the net.

"Goal, Blizzards! Number seven, Grant Buckley!" said the announcer. The crowd cheered.

After that, the second line subbed in. They kept the puck in the Vultures' zone, making their opponents play tougher defense. The Blizzards' second line was led by a center named Eric. They got a couple of shots off, but the Vultures' goalie stopped all of them.

The first period was nearly over by the time Simon and the rest of the fourth line got in the game. Simon felt even more nervous when he finally took the ice. He skated hard, but he always felt like he was two steps behind. Every time he had the puck, it was either swiped away from him or he was pinned against the boards by a Vultures' defender.

When Simon skated off the ice and back to the bench, he unstrapped his helmet and grumbled under his breath.

"Nice work out there, Simon," Coach said.

"Thanks," Simon said, but privately he thought, *You clearly aren't watching the game.*

In the second period, the Vultures scored three goals, taking the lead by two. That score held up until the final moments of the second period, when Grant snuck a wrist shot under the right leg of the Vultures' goalie.

The Zamboni rolled onto the ice as the buzzer marked the end of the second period, and the Blizzards hit the locker room. Simon, who was sweating like crazy, squirted a stream of water over his head before taking a huge drink from his water bottle.

"I hope I get another chance out there," he said to Quentin, who sat next to him retaping his stick. "They're skating circles around me."

"Listen up!" Coach Burke called from his position by the locker room door. "You're doing a great job of controlling the puck. Now you need to attack. Be aggressive, and don't back down. I don't want any penalties out there, though. Clean hits and smart plays. Are we clear?"

"Yes, sir," the team said in unison.

The Blizzards came out strong in the third period. Passes were crisp, and they had more shots on goal than in the first two periods combined. The Vultures did a great job on defense but gave up the tying goal when Quentin scored a tap-in after the puck bounced off the goalie's pads.

Late in the period, when Simon's line went into the game, the score was still tied at three.

Simon lined up for a face-off in the Blizzards' zone. When the referee dropped the puck, Simon slashed at it furiously.

The puck skittered away, then bounced off the board and back toward Simon. He cradled it, carving past a Vultures' player. Suddenly Simon was sailing down the center of the rink with one defender to beat. He faked to the left, then moved right. The Vultures' defender tried to pull up and change direction but couldn't.

Simon had a breakaway.

The Vultures' goalie skated forward, out of the crease, narrowing Simon's angle on the net. He had a split second to decide where to aim.

Left side of the net? Simon thought. *Or right?* He chose the left side. He brought his stick back and took aim, but suddenly, from out of nowhere, a Vultures' defender snuck in and knocked the puck off course.

No! Simon shouted internally. He turned, twisted his upper body, and searched angrily for the defender. He saw the player chasing the puck and took off after his opponent.

When he reached the defender, who had regained control of the puck, he slashed his stick at the opposing player out of sheer frustration. It sailed high on the Vultures' defender and clipped him across the right shoulder.

The ref blew his whistle. "Penalty for high-sticking," he shouted, pointing at Simon. "Two-minute minor."

Simon couldn't believe it. He'd let his emotions get the best of him, and now the Blizzards were going to be short one player for the next two minutes, giving the Vultures a power play. He skated to the penalty box, head hung low. The crowd mumbled, disappointed.

The Vultures took advantage of the penalty. One minute into the power play, they had a two-on-one breakaway toward the Blizzards' goal. One of their wingers slapped a shot past the Blizzards' goalie and straight into the net.

"Goal, Vultures!" the announcer called.

The Blizzards couldn't recover from Simon's mistake. When the buzzer echoed through the arena at the end of the game, the Blizzards had lost by a score of 4–3. And Simon knew he had just cost his team their opening home game.

CHAPTER 6

CRASH AND BURN

The next morning in science class, Simon's eyelids felt like they were made out of lead. He really should have been focusing on what Ms. Mayhew was writing on the whiteboard — something about the periodic table of elements. But all he could think about was sleep. Or rather, how little sleep he'd been getting lately.

Maybe I can just close my eyes for a second, Simon thought. *Just . . . for a . . . sec . . .*

"Psst! Hey, Simon! Wake up, man!" Mike whispered.

Simon peeled his eyes open, which took far more effort than he'd expected. Mike was at the right of his desk, and Kaya sat to his left. Simon could have sworn he'd just blinked. But he must have been asleep for a while, because there was a long line of drool hanging from the corner of his mouth, and it was quickly forming a small puddle on the desk.

"Ugh," Simon said, wiping the drool from his mouth with the sleeve of his sweatshirt. He looked up at the clock. "Wait, how long have I been —"

"A couple minutes," Mike answered. "But Ms. Mayhew looked over here once. I think she saw you snoozing."

"She's handing out our grades for the group project in a minute," Kaya added.

Oh yeah. I kind of forgot about that, Simon thought.

The truth was, he'd contributed very little to their report. After missing their group meeting

Saturday, Simon had told them he'd put in extra work at home. But he hadn't. His portion of the project — a report on velocity — had been thrown together in less than an hour on Sunday night — the night before the entire assignment was due.

But still, there was only one thing on Simon's mind — the Blizzards' loss the previous night. *Maybe I'm not cut out to play hockey for the Blizzards,* he thought. *I'm working so hard, but I keep getting the same results.*

"And now," Ms. Mayhew said, interrupting Simon's train of thought, "the moment you've all been waiting for." She picked up a stack of papers from her desk and began to pass them out. "Some of you did excellent work. Others . . ." Simon swore that Ms. Mayhew looked right at him, "showed room for improvement."

Simon had a sinking feeling. Sure enough, when Ms. Mayhew handed his group their papers, he saw a giant "D" on his portion of the project.

Mike and Kaya had each gotten an A-. Combined, their group grade was . . .

"We got a C+?" Mike said, shocked. "Oh, man. That's terrible."

"We worked so hard on it, too," Kaya added, looking at Mike.

Simon said nothing. He was too busy staring at the giant red "D" on his section of the report. *Not only did I cost my team the opening game, now I've let my friends down, too,* Simon thought. *I can't do anything right.*

* * *

After class, Simon waited for the other students to file out. Once they had all left, he approached Ms. Mayhew. She was writing chemical equations and notes about the periodic table on the whiteboard.

"Um, Ms. Mayhew?" Simon said.

The teacher turned to face him. "Ah, Mr. Wahlberg. How can I help you?"

The expression on his teacher's face made Simon believe she already knew what he was going to ask. He held out his report. "I just . . . well, I wanted to ask you if you'd consider changing my team's grade on the group project."

Ms. Mayhew shook her head. "I'm sorry, Simon. The grades reflect your team's work both individually and as a whole."

"I know," Simon said. "I was hoping you would consider . . . well, taking my grade off the team's grade."

"But you did the work with your team, did you not?" Ms. Mayhew asked.

"In class, yes. But . . ." Simon hesitated. "I've been working really hard at hockey, too. Our schedule doesn't really leave me a lot of time to do my homework."

"Well, that would explain your nodding off in class today," his teacher said, giving him a pointed look.

Simon's heart skipped a beat. Busted. "I'm okay with getting a D," he explained. "I deserved it. But I think Mike and Kaya deserve their individual grades as well."

Ms. Mayhew considered this for a moment. Then she said, "Here's my proposal to you, Simon. I won't remove your grade from the group, but I will give you another shot at helping your group out. You may have one week to rewrite your assignment. The grade you receive after that will be your final grade. Understood?"

Simon nodded his head vigorously. "Thank you, Ms. Mayhew," he said. "I won't let you down."

"And let me give you a word of advice for the future," Ms. Mayhew said. "I have nothing against succeeding at sports. But you need to find a balance, Simon. Your schoolwork cannot suffer because of your after-school activities."

"Yes, Ms. Mayhew," Simon said. Behind him, students began to file into the classroom and find their seats for the next class. The bell would ring soon, and he needed to get to his next class as soon as possible — to avoid getting into any more trouble.

"Hurry along, then," Ms. Mayhew said. "I'm looking forward to reading your report."

Simon smiled, then turned and darted out of the room, weaving through the halls on his way to his next class.

CHAPTER 7

DECISION TIME

That afternoon, the Blizzards started practice by skating laps around the ice rink. Simon couldn't stop thinking about what Ms. Mayhew had said. He had let down his group. He had been focusing too much of his time on hockey, and now his grades were paying the price for it.

And the worst part? Simon thought. *Hockey isn't even fun anymore. I'm actually bored when I'm playing. I feel like I've lost all of my passion, and I don't know how I'm ever going to get it —*

"Whoa! Head's up!" someone shouted.

Simon was so lost in thought that he hadn't noticed he was skating right at Blake until it was too late. He clipped the other player with his right shoulder, and their skates tangled. The two boys went down hard on the ice.

Simon quickly scrambled to his knees. "Oh, man," he said, moving toward Blake. "I am so sorry. Are you okay?"

Blake groaned. "Yeah, I'm good," he said, but it was clear that the wind had been knocked out of him.

"Everything all right over here?" Coach Burke, not wearing skates, slid across the ice in his sneakers. Coach Martin was behind him.

"Wahlberg wasn't paying attention," someone muttered. Simon turned and saw Grant. He hadn't realized the team captain was standing right behind him.

Coach Martin helped Blake to his feet. Blake shook his head as if he was clearing out some cobwebs. "Man," he said. "I haven't been checked that hard all season."

"I'm so sorry, Blake," Simon said, helping him off the ice.

Simon felt horrible. He was starting to think that he would be better off forgetting all about hockey.

And that really scared him.

* * *

On the ride home from practice, Simon sat with his forehead pressed against the cool window. He stared out at nothing in particular while his dad listened to one of the broadcasters from the local sports radio station drone on about the woes of this season's football team.

Finally, Dad reached out and turned the radio off. "How was practice?" he asked.

Simon shrugged. "Okay, I guess."

"Big game against Maple Plains on Saturday," Dad noted. "They haven't lost a game yet."

Maple Plains High School, home of the Wolves, was Edgewater's biggest rival. The whole student body came to the game. Some of the local news stations even picked it up.

"Do you think you guys will be able to beat them?" Dad asked.

"Hopefully," Simon said halfheartedly.

His dad's brow furrowed with concern. "Is everything okay?"

Simon had never kept any secrets from his dad. But this time, he felt like he couldn't tell his dad the truth. He didn't want to tell him about the D he'd gotten on his report. And he certainly didn't want to tell him how much he'd been struggling with hockey.

After everything Mom and Dad have given up so that I could transfer to Edgewater and play for the Blizzards . . . how can I tell them I don't enjoy hockey anymore? Simon wondered.

Instead, he said, "Yeah, everything's fine."

"Mmhmm," Dad said.

Simon could tell his dad wasn't buying it.

When they were close to home, Dad took a detour. They wound up at the park, pulling up to the curb right next to the man-made rink, which was now filled with ice. It was lit by a single streetlight, which cast the rink in a bluish glow. Surprisingly, it was empty.

"What are you doing?" Simon asked. "Isn't Mom waiting for us to help make dinner?"

"Dinner can wait," Dad said, popping the car's trunk and killing the engine. "Let's grab our skates from the back."

* * *

"Now this is what it's all about," Dad said several minutes later as he skated along the edge of the man-made rink. The ice was filled with grooves and ridges from previous skaters. "A cold night, an outdoor rink, and a pair of ice skates. It's pretty much everything a guy could ask for."

Simon leaned against the plywood boards that circled the rink and watched his dad — every turn, every twist, every two-skated stop that sent ice shavings flying into the air. There was such joy in his movements and on his face.

Simon tried to remember what it was like to feel that way. At his old school, there hadn't been any of the pressure he felt here. Hockey had been easy back then, and Simon had been the star of the team.

After making a few laps around the rink, Simon's dad came to a stop. "So," he said, "you ready to tell me what's really eating you?"

Simon sighed. It was no use. The truth weighed heavily on him, and pretending like everything was just fine wasn't working.

"I think I'm going to quit the team," Simon said quickly. "Hockey isn't fun like it used to be. I try so hard at practice, but I always mess up. I never have time for anything else because I'm always at practice or worrying about the next game. I don't hang out with friends outside of the team, I hardly have time to do homework —"

"Whoa, whoa. School, friends, family . . . those things are more important, Simon," Dad interrupted.

Simon sighed. "That's just it," he said. "School. I wanted to tell you this before, but . . . promise you won't be mad?"

"Promise," Dad replied.

"Well," Simon began, "I got a bad grade on a group science report. My first D."

Simon wasn't sure how his dad would react.

The last thing I want to do is disappoint my parents, he thought. *I would understand if Dad's upset with me and if he thinks I'm giving up too easily . . . on hockey and on schoolwork.*

"Oh," was all his dad said. Then, after a moment of silence, he asked, "How long has all this been going on?"

"I dunno. A few weeks now, I guess," Simon admitted.

"And you weren't going to talk to me about it?" Dad asked.

"There's just so much pressure," Simon said. "From the team, from my coaches, from school. I thought I'd get better at balancing schoolwork and hockey. I thought if I kept at it on the ice, there would be a spark . . . something that made hockey fun again. Plus, I didn't want to let you down or disappoint you and Mom."

Simon's dad pinched his lips closed and exhaled loudly. "Simon," he said, frowning. "The last thing in the world I could possibly be is disappointed by you."

Simon looked down at the ice and toed it with one skate. "Thanks," he said.

"I will support whatever decision you make," Dad continued. "Your schoolwork comes first, though. So if you want to find a way to continue playing hockey with the Blizzards, you'll also need to focus on your grades. And if you want to quit hockey altogether, or wait a year or two and try out again, I'm behind you one hundred percent."

"Okay," Simon said quietly. "Thanks, Dad."

"You bet, kiddo."

Simon pushed off from the board, gliding toward the center of the rink.

Sure, I'll miss hockey at first, Simon thought. *But I'm not having fun the way I used to. For now, at least, I need a break.*

Simon decided to tell his coach he wouldn't be joining the team the next day for practice . . . or for any practice for the rest of the season.

The weight that had been sitting so firmly on Simon's shoulders just a moment ago was now gone. He twisted around, skating backward, easily looping his way across the ice.

He felt like he was skating on air.

CHAPTER 8

LAST PRACTICE

"Coach?" Simon said before practice the next morning, peeking his head around the office door. "There's something I'd like to talk to you about."

It took every bit of Simon's courage to face Coach Burke and tell him he was quitting the team. Practice was starting in ten minutes, and most of the guys were already on the ice. Simon, however, was still in his street clothes. His hands were shoved deep in the front pocket of his hooded sweatshirt, where he was nervously wringing them together, trying to get them to stop shaking.

Coach Burke sat in the locker room's small, cluttered office. He looked up at Simon, who stood in the doorway. "What can I do for you, Simon?"

Simon felt a lump form in his throat. He cleared it out and said, "I just . . . I want to talk to you about, well, about my future with the team."

Coach Burke sat back, and his old padded metal chair creaked. "Well," he said, "I would be happy to talk with you. How about after practice?"

Simon's shoulders slumped. He didn't want to go to practice. "Coach Burke," he said, "I kind of hoped we could talk right now."

Coach stood, gathering his things. It was pretty clear that he didn't want to have a conversation right then. "Suit up," he said. "Big practice this morning. I've got a feeling you'll like it."

Simon sighed. Clearly he was going to practice whether he liked it or not. "Um . . . all right," he said. Trudging over to his locker, he got dressed for a practice he didn't want to attend.

A few minutes later, Simon joined the team on the ice. They gathered around Coach Burke at center ice. Coach Martin stood beside Coach Burke with a bunch of blue jerseys in his left hand and a bunch of yellow ones in his right.

"Pretty sure I don't have to tell you, but our game against Maple Plains on Saturday will be the toughest of the season," Coach Burke said.

"Oh, they're going down," Blake said. Some of the other Blizzards loudly agreed, whooping and hollering to show their support.

"I've decided to shake some things up for the game," Coach Burke said. "Change up the lines a bit. Many of you have been working really hard out there, and I want to reward that passion."

Grant seemed confused. "Why are we mixing things up *now*?" he asked.

Coach Burke shrugged. "Why not?" There was a twinkle in his eye. "First line — Grant, Quentin, and Eric." Each of them was given a yellow jersey.

But wait, Simon thought. *Eric is the second line's center. If he's not on the second line, who's —*

"Simon, you're going to be our second-line center in our game against Maple Plains on Saturday. Blake and Kent, you'll be at the wings," Coach said.

What? Simon thought. *I'm going to be the second-line center?* He could hardly believe it. The news was so surprising that when Coach Martin tossed him a blue jersey, Simon almost dropped it.

"Look who's moved up in the world!" Blake said to Simon with a grin.

Kent, who had kept his position as right wing on the second line, high-fived a bewildered Simon.

The second-line offense was made up of strong players who added a scoring boost to the first line. The fact that Coach Burke had placed him at center showed he believed Simon could lead the offense and score some goals. In an instant, Simon's role on the team had changed significantly.

"All right, let's line up and scrimmage. I want to see our new first line versus second line to begin!" Coach Burke shouted. "And for crying out loud, have a little fun out there!"

Simon skated to face-off circle where Grant was already waiting. Grant usually intimidated him, but Simon was filled with a renewed drive.

When Grant scowled at him, Simon just chuckled and muttered, "Bring it on, Buckley."

Coach Martin dropped a puck between Grant and Simon. Grant won the face-off, but that didn't surprise Simon.

Grant slapped the puck over to Quentin, who hung back instead of driving into the zone right away. Quentin liked to take his time, looking for the best place to strike. Finally, Quentin slipped the puck forward to Eric.

Eric skated fast along the right side, gliding past a defender. But before he could get a shot off, Blake intercepted Eric, knocking him into the boards. A defender cleared the puck out to the neutral zone.

Simon gobbled it up, turned, and broke toward the net. Grant was skating up hard on his left. Simon edged him out, skating faster than he ever imagined he could.

He broke past Howie, lined up, and swung with confidence. The puck sliced through the air, found a gap between Nate's arm and leg, and hit the net.

"Goal!" Blake shouted. "Unassisted!"

Simon's heart raced as his line surrounded him, slapping his pads and helmet in celebration.

"Center ice!" Coach Burke hollered excitedly. "Let's go again!"

The scrimmage went on for nearly an hour. Players hooted, cheering one another on after each goal. At the end of the scrimmage, Simon wound up with two goals and three assists.

The teams lined up to bump fists like they would after a game. Simon received praise from most of the guys. In fact, even Grant had something kind to say. "Nice skating out there," he mumbled as they bumped fists.

"Thanks," Simon said, surprised. "You, too."

Simon didn't want it to be over. The scrimmage, his goals — they were exhilarating. It was the spark Simon had been looking for, the one that might trigger his love for hockey once again.

I'm going to be on the second line for the Maple Plains game? Simon still couldn't believe it.

As Simon changed in the locker room, which was still buzzing with excitement for the upcoming game, some of his teammates congratulated him.

When he was just about to leave, Coach Burke approached him and said, "Wahlberg, wasn't there something you wanted to talk to me about earlier?"

Simon shook his head. "Nope. Nothing at all, Coach."

Coach Burke smiled. "I didn't think so. Great practice, kid."

CHAPTER 9

GAME ON

It was Saturday, the morning of the big game against Maple Plains, and Simon was nervous. He drummed his fingers against the kitchen table while his mom made his favorite breakfast — waffles topped with strawberries, maple syrup, and finally some whipped cream. Healthy? No. But delicious? No doubt.

His mom slid a heaping plate of waffles, along with a plate of bacon and a tall glass of orange juice, in front of him at the kitchen table. Simon noticed that she was already wearing a Blizzards' sweatshirt with a giant pin of Simon's team photo attached to it.

Mom ruffled his already mussed hair and said, "Good luck today, honey. We'll be there rooting for you."

"Thanks, Mom," Simon said around a mouthful of waffles.

Simon was anxious for the game to start. He made it to the locker room earlier than his entire team — coaches included — that morning. It was the most excited he'd felt about hockey in a very long time.

While he waited for his teammates to arrive, Simon plugged in a set of earbuds, lay back on the wooden bench in front of his locker, and listened to some music. He shut his eyes and daydreamed about the different ways the Blizzards could win the big game.

At last, the wait was over. Simon's teammates showed up, followed by Coach Burke and Coach

Martin. Simon suited up, taking extra care putting on his shoulder pads and skates.

With the puck drop only thirty minutes away, Coach Burke herded the team out of the locker room. As each player passed, Coach smacked him on the shoulder pads and shouted words of encouragement.

The crowd was the largest of the season. The whole arena was packed with fans. Many wore Blizzards' blue and yellow. The Edgewater pep band was present, and they filled the rink with music so loud it seemed to bounce off the walls.

Maple Plains had been Edgewater's biggest rival for more than fifty years, and each season, the game drew major attention. Some local news stations had even come to film game highlights. There was a section for the reporters down near the rink.

"First line! Let's go!" Coach Burke shouted after warm-ups and player introductions. The team swarmed around the bench, banging their sticks against the boards, getting each other pumped up.

Grant took center ice. The Maple Plains center skated up across from him. The referee blew the whistle, dropped the puck, and the game was on.

The Wolves won the face-off, taking the puck into the Blizzards' zone. They were aggressive and not afraid to take shots. Nate blocked three shots in a row, all within a few minutes of one another. On the fourth shot, the puck hit his left leg, and he covered it with his giant mitt.

On the next face-off, Grant cleared the puck from the Blizzards' zone, giving Nate time to catch his breath.

The first line battled fiercely. When Coach Burke yelled, "Second line! You're in!" across the bench, the score was still tied at zero.

Simon's heart raced. It felt like it might burst through his pads.

This is it! he thought.

The first line skated toward the bench. Simon and the others hopped over the boards, subbing into the game in the middle of the action. Simon's skates hit the ice, and he was off.

Kent made it to the puck first. He swiped it from a Wolves' winger, checking the opposing player into the boards. Then he passed the puck to Blake, who crossed center ice with it.

Simon raced along on Blake's left. Blake passed to him, drawing the defenders toward Simon, who skated furiously behind the net. When he came around to the other side, Simon spotted Blake open in front of the net. He quickly slipped a pass across the ice. Blake wound up and . . .

Crack!

The shot echoed through the loud arena, making the fans go quiet for a moment. The puck found a gap, passed by the goalie's mitt, and struck the net.

A siren sounded, and the announcer said, "Goal, Blizzards! Number forty-four, Blake Vaughn."

When the third line subbed in, Simon and Blake skated to the bench together. As they climbed over the boards, Simon said, "Man, this is what it's all about. Am I right?"

Blake smiled. "You know it."

Maple Plains wasn't undefeated for no reason, though. The Wolves weren't going to give up easily. Barely a minute into the second period they scored to tie the game. By the end of the period, both Grant and the Wolves' center had each scored a goal, keeping the score tied at two.

It stayed that way through most of the third period. When he was on the ice, Simon skated like he never had before.

With less than a minute left in the game, Simon and the rest of the second line were on the ice. If neither team scored, they would have a shoot-out. But Simon was determined not to let that happen.

He was nearly exhausted of energy. His breath burned in his throat. But still, he pressed forward. Simon watched as the puck skittered along the boards on the far side of the rink, heading toward the Edgewater zone. He raced over to it.

As Simon caught the puck with the blade of his stick, a Wolves' player checked him hard into the boards, knocking the air out of his lungs. Pain tore down his side. It felt like he'd been hit by a cement truck.

But Simon wasn't going to let the puck go that easily. He shot forward, scooping up the puck and passing it back to where Kent was waiting. Kent sent the puck across the zone to Blake as Simon pushed off the boards, lowering his head and skating forward.

Blake saw him speeding along and zipped the puck up to him. Simon came to an abrupt stop. Ice shavings exploded into the air. He wound up and swung.

The puck whistled through the air . . . right into the net.

"Goal, Blizzards!" the announcer called. "Number eleven, Simon Wahlberg!"

Simon couldn't believe it. He stared at the net in disbelief. The goal siren and lights blared, and the crowd went nuts.

Blake grabbed Simon in a bear hug. "Nice shot, dude!" he shouted. Simon could barely hear him over the noise of the crowd.

There were still thirty seconds left in the game. Down by one, the Wolves pulled their goalie and tried desperately to score, taking shot after shot. The Blizzards put up a strong defense, though, and when the final buzzer rang through the arena, Simon's goal was the difference.

The final score was 3–2. The Blizzards had won!

The band played the Edgewater school song as the crowd in the stands thinned. Reporters from local TV stations swarmed the ice and pulled players from both teams aside to ask questions.

A woman in a bright blue puffy coat with her station's logo on it approached Simon. "Mind if I ask you a question?" she asked.

Her cameraman shouldered his camera. A light perched atop the camera shined brightly in Simon's eyes.

"Uh, yeah," Simon said, squinting into the light. "Sure."

"Great. How does it feel score a goal and help your team to such a big win?" the reporter asked.

Simon thought about all of the people who would see him on the news. Panic nearly seized him. But then he thought about how amazing the whole night had been, and how much he loved hockey. "It's the best feeling in the world!" he said.

CHAPTER 10

WIN-WIN

The following Monday, Simon sat in science class nervously tapping his fingers on his desk and waiting for Ms. Mayhew to hand back his report. Again.

But this time was different. Simon had spent a lot of time studying before rewriting his report on velocity. In fact, he'd spent most of the weekend, aside from the hockey game, working on the assignment.

Ms. Mayhew was sitting at her desk, staring at her computer monitor. Her fingers danced quickly across her keyboard. Suddenly, she stopped typing and stood up.

Simon's pulse quickened. He didn't want to let his group down again. Ms. Mayhew plucked a stack of papers off her desk and began walking toward him.

The teacher stopped beside his desk, and Simon's nerves went into overdrive. "Mr. Wahlberg?" she said.

Simon tried to act cool. He failed. "Yes, Ms. Mayhew?" The words barely squeaked out.

She held out the paper. "Nice work." A smirk, an honest-to-goodness smirk, flitted briefly across her face. Proof that Ms. Mayhew actually smiled once in a while.

It's like catching a glimpse of Bigfoot or something, Simon thought.

Simon looked at the red marking on the top of his paper. In Ms. Mayhew's looping cursive were the words, "Congratulations. A-."

"How'd you do?" Mike whispered from behind him. He was trying to crane his neck to see over Simon's shoulder.

"An A-," Simon said. He was so excited he wanted to jump up onto his desk and break out in a celebratory dance. His grade felt about as amazing as scoring a hat trick.

"Hey," Simon whispered to his friends after getting over the shock. "Do you guys want to come over after school to celebrate and go ice skating at the park?"

Kaya and Mike both smiled. "Sure!" they said.

* * *

"I can't believe I'm doing this," Kaya said that afternoon as she laced up her skates beside the man-made rink at the park. "I've never been on ice skates before."

"How is it that you live in Minnesota but you've never been on ice skates?" Mike asked.

"You'll do great," Simon said encouragingly.

Simon felt sorry for letting them down in the beginning, but he was glad he'd been able to make it up to them — and to himself — with the new and improved grade on his portion of the group project.

Simon took Kaya's hand and helped her out onto the ice. Kaya wobbled a bit, letting out a brief shriek as she almost fell. With Simon's help, though, she managed to stay upright.

"This is awesome," Mike said. He skated in wide circles. He wasn't an expert, but he certainly wasn't a novice. "Thanks for inviting us, Simon."

"Absolutely," Simon said. "Sorry I almost ruined your science grades."

Mike waved a hand dismissively at him. "I knew you'd come through."

A car horn honked twice, and Simon turned around to see a green Jeep parked at the curb. A few of Simon's teammates — Grant, Blake, and Quentin — hopped out.

"Hey, guys!" Simon called.

"'Sup, Simon," Quentin said.

"What's going on?" Simon asked.

"Well," Grant said, "we've got another big game coming up this Friday. We figured we should probably be practicing."

"Oh," Simon said. "Yeah. You guys headed over to the rink? Because I'm planning on hanging out with these guys today."

Grant reached into the front seat of his Jeep and pulled out a pair of ice skates. "Nah," he said. "We'd rather join you guys, if that's cool."

Simon looked over at Kaya and Mike, gauging their reaction to Grant's offer. Mike gave him a thumbs-up.

"The more, the merrier," Kaya said.

"So," Blake said, smiling, "what do you say? Mind if we join your party?"

Simon grinned back. "Yeah," he answered. "That sounds like fun."

ABOUT THE AUTHOR

Brandon Terrell is the author of numerous children's books, including several volumes in both the Tony Hawk 900 Revolution series and the Tony Hawk Live 2 Skate series, graphic novels for Sports Illustrated Kids, chapter books, and a picture book about trains. When not hunched over his laptop writing, Brandon enjoys watching movies and television, reading, watching (and playing!) baseball, and spending time with his wife and two children in Minnesota.

GLOSSARY

abrupt (uh-BRUPT)—sudden and unexpected

aggressive (uh-GRESS-iv)—ready and willing to fight

confidence (KAHN-fi-duhns)—a strong belief in one's own abilities

exhilerating (eg-ZIL-uh-ray-ting)—very exciting

flitted (FLIT-id)—moved quickly and lightly

frustrated (FRUHS-tray-tid)—felt discouraged

hypothesis (hye-POTH-uh-siss)—an idea that could explain how something works but that has to be tested through experiments to be proven right

intercepted (in-tur-SEP-tid)—stopped the movement of someone or something

passion (PASH-uhn)—great devotion or enthusiasm; a very strong feeling

undefeated (un-dih-FEET-id)—if a team is undefeated, they haven't lost a game throughout the entire season

DISCUSSION QUESTIONS

1. Why do you think Simon begins to question his love for hockey? Talk about the things that might have discouraged Simon when he joined his new team.

2. Imagine you are Mike or Kaya. How would you have felt about Simon missing your meetings for the science project? Talk about how your feelings might have changed when he rewrote his part of the report.

3. What are some things Simon could have done to better balance schoolwork, hockey, and friends? Talk about some possibilities.

GUNNISON COUNTY LIBRARY DISTRICT

Ann Zugelder Library
307 N. Wisconsin Gunnison, CO 81230
970.641.3485
www.gunnisoncountylibraries.org

WRITING PROMPTS

1. Simon has a hard time deciding whether or not he should stay on the Blizzards. Pretend you are Simon and write a list of pros and cons to help you make your decision.

2. When Simon's group gets a bad grade on their science report, Mike and Kaya are upset. Write about a time someone let you down. How did it make you feel?

3. Imagine you are Coach Burke. Write a letter to Simon encouraging him to stick with hockey. Make sure to include advice for succeeding both on and off the ice.

More About
ICE HOCKEY

The first modern indoor ice hockey game was played in **MONTREAL, CANADA,** in 1875, but variations of the sport have been around for much longer than that.

While the origins of ice hockey are not entirely known, some people think it may have been adapted from **FIELD HOCKEY**, a popular game in Europe throughout the nineteenth and twentieth centuries.

The game of **LACROSSE,** originally played by Native Americans, may have influenced the sport of modern ice hockey as well.